MW00909792

Merida
Is Our Babysitter

By Apple Jordan
Illustrated by Mario Cortés and Meritxell Andreu

 A GOLDEN BOOK • NEW YORK

Copyright © 2016 Disney Enterprises, Inc. All rights reserved.
Published in the United States by Golden Books, an imprint of Random House Children's Books,
a division of Penguin Random House LLC, 1745 Broadway, New York, NY 10019, and in Canada
by Penguin Random House Canada Limited, Toronto, in conjunction with Disney Enterprises,
Inc. Golden Books, A Golden Book, A Little Golden Book, the G colophon, and the distinctive
gold spine are registered trademarks of Penguin Random House LLC.

randomhousekids.com

ISBN 978-0-7364-3614-4 (trade) — ISBN 978-0-7364-3615-1 (ebook)

Printed in the United States of America

10 9 8 7 6 5 4 3 2

One day, Queen Elinor and King Fergus were getting ready to attend a royal banquet. Maudie the nursemaid had the day off, so Merida was going to babysit her brothers for the first time.

"They can be quite a handful," Merida's mother warned.

"I can manage the wee ones," Merida assured her parents. "Don't worry about a thing."

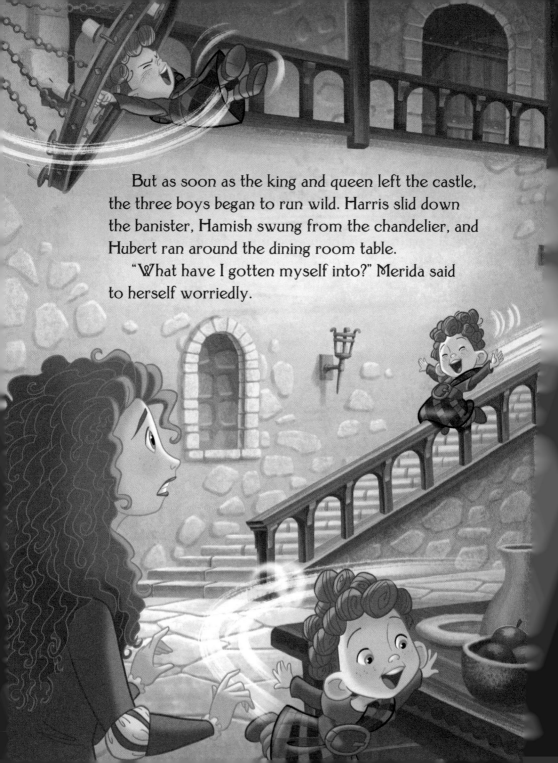

But as soon as the king and queen left the castle, the three boys began to run wild. Harris slid down the banister, Hamish swung from the chandelier, and Hubert ran around the dining room table.

"What have I gotten myself into?" Merida said to herself worriedly.

She quickly thought of a plan to keep her brothers busy—and out of trouble!

"Let's have an archery contest," she suggested.

Outside, Merida watched as each boy held up his arrow and pulled back his bow.

"One . . . two . . . three!" she counted. The boys released their arrows. Harris's and Hamish's arrows each landed in the bull's-eye.

But Hubert's arrow went too high and pierced an apple in the tree above them! The apple landed right on one of the queen's favorite garden statues. Merida caught the statue just before it fell to the ground.

"Phew! That was close," said Merida. "Maybe we should do something else."

The boys were getting restless again. Merida had
to think of another activity fast.

"Let's check on the horses," she said. The triplets
ran off excitedly to the stable.

Hubert gathered some hay for the horses. Hamish filled the trough with fresh water. And Harris combed the horses' tails. WHAT A MESS!

Before the triplets could get into any more trouble, Merida suggested they saddle up the horses and take a long ride.

"This should keep them busy for a while," she said to herself.

When they stopped to give their horses a drink from
a stream, the boys noticed a trail of glowing blue lights.
Hamish jumped up and ran after them. His brothers
followed. The three boys tried to catch the tiny blue fairies.
"Leave them be," Merida warned. "If you chase the will
o' the wisps, they'll lead you astray and get you lost."

The boys didn't listen. Instead, they got on their
horses and galloped after the wisps.

"Come back!" Merida called. But they were already
gone. She jumped on her horse and chased them.

Merida followed the boys into the woods. Soon they were out of sight.

She came to a fork in the path. She didn't know which way the boys had turned.

Merida began to worry. "Where could those rascals be?"

Merida saw the wisps fluttering ahead. They seemed to be waiting for her, so she followed them.

The blue fairies led her deeper into the forest. Finally, they stopped at the bottom of a large pine tree.

Merida looked up. There were her three brothers, stuck high in the branches!

"Now do you believe me?" Merida called to the boys. "Those wisps are mischief-makers!"

The triplets were kicking and fussing to be rescued.

Merida helped them down. "Well, those pesky wisps can't be all bad," she said. "They did come back to help me find you."

When she turned around to thank the fairies, they were gone.

Back at the castle, Merida found more ways
to keep her brothers busy. They helped prepare
dinner—a feast fit for three wee kings!

Then they cleared the table, washed the dishes,
and mopped the floor.

At last it was time for bed. The boys changed into their pajamas, brushed their teeth, and then ran to find a bedtime story.

The triplets each had a favorite book, and they bickered about which one Merida would read first.

"Don't worry," said Merida. "I'll read *all* your stories. Now settle down."

But the princess was exhausted from her busy day. Before she could finish the first page of the first book, her eyes closed.

The boys gently placed a blanket over their sister. Then they snuggled in close and fell asleep.

When Queen Elinor and King Fergus returned home, they found Merida and her brothers fast asleep.

"See? I told you there was nothing to worry about," said the king. "MERIDA IS THE PERFECT BABYSITTER!"